Hi there,

I'm David Warner, Australian cricketer,
and I'm really excited to introduce you to
my new series of kids' books called
The Kaboom Kid.

Little Davey Warner is 'the Kaboom Kid',
a cricket-mad eleven-year-old who wants to
play cricket with his mates every minute of
the day, just like I did as a kid.

Davey gets into all sorts of scrapes with his
friends, but mainly he has a great time playing
cricket for his cricket club, the Sandhill Sluggers,
and helping them win lots of matches.

If you're into cricket, and I know you are, then you
will love these books. Enjoy *The Kaboom Kid*.

David Warner

THE KABOOM KID

Keep It Down!

DAVID WARNER

with J. V. MCGEE, Illustrated by JULES FABER

SIMON & SCHUSTER
AUSTRALIA
A CBS COMPANY

THE KABOOM KID: KEEP IT DOWN!
First published in Australia in 2015 by
Simon & Schuster (Australia) Pty Limited
Suite 19A, Level 1, 450 Miller Street, Cammeray, NSW 2062

10 9 8 7 6 5 4 3 2 1

A CBS Company
Sydney New York London Toronto New Delhi
Visit our website at www.simonandschuster.com.au

© David Warner and J.V. McGee 2015

National Library of Australia Cataloguing-in-Publication entry

Creator:	Warner, David Andrew, author.
Title:	The kaboom kid: keep it down!/David Warner and J.V. McGee.
ISBN:	9781925030822 (paperback)
	9781925030839 (ebook)
Target Audience:	For children.
Subjects:	Warner, David Andrew.
	Cricket–Australia–Juvenile literature.
	Cricket players–Australia–Juvenile literature.
	Cricket–Batting–Juvenile literature.
Other Authors/	
Contributors:	McGee, J. V., author.
Dewey Number:	796.3580994

Cover and internal design by Hannah Janzen
Cover and internal illustrations by Jules Faber
Inside cover photograph of adult David Warner by © Quinn Rooney/Getty Images
Typeset by Midland Typesetters, Australia
Printed and bound in India by Replika Press Pvt. Ltd.

FOR CANDICE

FOR ZANDILE

CONTENTS

CHAPTER 1

ELEVEN GREEN BATTERS . . .

'Warner, you're reserve keeper!' Sunil Deep was speaking in his team captain's voice, even though they were just having a hit in the playground before school.

'Aye, aye, cap'n.' Davey Warner bowed and doffed the old trucker's cap he called his baggy

green, but he wasn't exactly ecstatic as he trudged to the spot behind the wicket.

'It's not my thing,' he said to his friend, George Pepi, who was at the crease, bat in hand, waiting for Sunil to bowl. 'Batting – yep, definitely. A bit of spin bowling – if I'm needed. But wicket-keeping?' He shook his head.

Sunil ran in and bowled a fast ball on leg stump. George hit it off the front foot straight to mid-on. Ivy Mundine was there, and she quickly got her hands to the ball and threw it back. George didn't try for a run.

'Yeah, well, as soon as Dylan turns up you're free,' George said. He frowned. 'His mum must have forgotten to wake him up again.'

Dylan was often late. He told his friends it was his mum's fault, but Davey had noticed

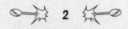

that Dylan's mum always seemed to be on time for parent–teacher interviews and when she had to see Mrs Trundle, the school principal, about Dylan breaking school rules again.

Still, nobody really minded. Dylan was one of those kids everyone liked – everyone except Mrs Trundle and their teacher, Mr Mudge.

With an invisible bat, Davey slogged an invisible ball for six. 'I wish he'd hurry up. I need a bit more time at the crease.' A real ball whizzed past his ear and George took the opportunity to run for a bye, bringing Kevin McNab, another of Davey's good friends, on to strike.

'What're you doing, Warner?' Sunil shouted. 'You're supposed to be keeping wicket, not pretending you're batting for Australia!'

Max, Davey's dog, was fielding at deep fine leg, even though Mrs Trundle had banned him from the school grounds for life. Now he chased the ball and, moments later, dropped it at Sunil's feet.

'I have to practise my shots for Friday,' Davey shouted. 'First game of the school comp. We've *got* to beat the Batfish!'

The last time Sandhill Flats Primary played Batfish Beach Primary they'd lost. Now they were thirsty for revenge.

Kevin nodded. 'Yep, gotta get those Batfish back.'

'You're a batfish!'

It was Mo Clouter, school bully and cricket detester. He and his friends Nero and Tony had wandered down to C playground to

4

look for something to do. They'd found it – bothering the cricketers was one of their favourite pastimes. Now they were standing right behind Davey, talking loudly and whistling, trying to put him off his game.

Davey tried to block them out. He focused on Sunil, who let loose a fast bouncer down the pitch.

Davey then Kevin ducked as the ball flew over their heads and sailed past Mo and his friends. 'Hey, watch what you're doing, Deep!' Mo shouted.

Sunil gave them a friendly wave. 'Sorry! Better get out of the way!'

But Mo didn't move. 'Hey, Shorty!' he called to Davey. 'Guess you'll have to be wicket-keeper from here on, now that Dylan's gone . . .'

Davey and Kevin glanced at each other.

'He's just late,' Davey shouted over his shoulder.

'Ha-ha!'

Davey turned around. Mo and his friends were holding their bellies and laughing like they'd just watched the funniest YouTube video ever.

Davey shook his head. 'What?'

'Yeah, three years late by the time you see him again. He's left. His whole family's gone. Didn't he tell you?'

Davey and the rest of the cricket team looked at each other. Dylan gone? Without telling them? He'd never do that.

'I don't believe it,' Davey said, turning his back on Mo and his crew.

'You'll find out soon enough!' Mo said. 'Right, guys?'

'Right!' Nero and Tony echoed.

'Dylan's gone, Shorty. His mum got some big job in a mine up north and they've moved. I heard Mrs Trundle tell Mudge last week.' Mo made a sad face. 'Guess he forgot to mention it to you.'

Mo and his fellow comedians lumbered off, laughing loudly.

Davey and the rest of the team stopped playing to discuss this latest piece of information.

'Do you reckon he's telling the truth?' George asked.

Sunil shrugged. 'Dunno. Dylan was off sick all last week. Maybe he was going to tell us then, but couldn't.'

Kevin stuck out his bottom lip. 'Hope it's not true. Who's gonna drive Mrs Trundle round the banana? Dylan's so-o-o-o good at that.'

They all nodded silently. Dylan had been an expert when it came to infuriating Mrs Trundle. He only had to step onto school grounds and wherever she was her eye would start twitching. It was fantastic to watch.

Davey felt a surge of fear rise in his stomach. If it *was* true – and it probably wasn't, because Mo was always making stuff up – Davey would miss Dylan, no doubt about it.

But, truth be told, that wasn't what Davey was most worried about. The surge of fear he felt was because, if Dylan *had* left, both the school team and the club cricket team would be without a wicket-keeper. Even worse, as reserve keeper, Davey would have to take on the job, at least until a substitute could be found. Which meant that at training he'd be spending too much time behind the wicket and less time at the crease. Worst of all, with the game coming up on Friday against Batfish Beach, Davey would most definitely have to keep wicket. Which he wasn't at all prepared for.

'Clouter's making it up,' Davey said. 'Dylan'll be here any minute.' But even though he tried to sound confident, the awful feeling didn't go away.

The school bell sounded. Max barked and tried to make a dash for it, but Davey caught him by the collar. 'You better get out of here before Trundle sees you,' he said, tugging the dog to the school gate.

Davey pushed Max through and surveyed the street. A few stragglers were still arriving to school, but there was no sign of Dylan.

Surely he wouldn't leave without saying goodbye, Davey thought. *And surely he wouldn't leave before the big match against the Batfish. Surely . . .*

CHAPTER 2

THE B4U FAN

Mr Mudge, the grumpiest teacher at Sandhill Flats Primary, stood in the doorway of the classroom and waved the students of 6M through. It was only 9.30 in the morning, but he already looked tired.

'Maybe Dylan's on the run?' Davey whispered loudly to Sunil as they squeezed past their teacher. Davey had recently seen a movie about a guy who'd been wrongly accused of something and everyone was after him. Maybe that had happened to Dylan, he thought, although he had to admit that when Dylan was accused of something he was usually guilty.

Sunil made a face. 'Yeah, well, Mrs Trundle's probably after him. But I don't think that's why he's not here.'

'If you're wondering where Dylan is, he's *moved*. Left on the weekend.' Mr Mudge sounded pleased.

Davey and Sunil looked at each other. So it was true. Dylan had gone. 'You'll have to be keeper, Warner. It's just the way it is,' Sunil whispered, before making his way to his seat in the far corner of the room.

Davey took his place near Bella Ferosi and Mo Clouter, in the opposite corner of the room from Sunil. Kevin and George occupied the other two corners. Mr Mudge's tactic of separating the four boys so they couldn't talk about cricket in class was certainly effective.

Mrs Trundle appeared in the doorway. Beside her was a tall girl with a long dark plait.

'Mrs Trundle!' Mr Mudge was grinning like a crocodile. 'Who do we have here?'

'Mr Mudge, 6M . . .' Mrs Trundle ushered the girl in. 'This is Tay Tui. She's new at our school. Tay doesn't know anyone here yet, so please introduce yourselves. I want everyone in Year Six to make her welcome.'

'I know Mo,' the new girl said in a clear voice. 'He's the cousin of my second-best friend, Shania.'

Mr Mudge smiled again. His ears, which changed colour to match his mood, were a rosy pink. 'Well, that's wonderful! Perhaps Mo can be your buddy for a while.' He looked across at the great galumph slumped in the chair beside Davey.

Mo nodded angelically. 'Sure, Sir. Shania's my favourite cousin.'

'In that case, Tay, we might sit you near Mo. He can help you settle in.'

Mr Mudge glanced at Bella Ferosi, school captain and 6M's most outstanding student. 'Bella, would you mind moving places? You can take Dylan's old spot.'

'I'd be happy to, Mr Mudge,' Bella said, smiling pleasantly and giving her ponytail a flick. In a split second, she'd packed up her belongings, dusted down the desk and moved to Dylan's place, right beside Kevin.

Davey looked at his friend with sympathy. Sitting next to Bella should have had its advantages, but Davey had never been able to copy any of her work because she always kept it well covered. She also always reported him to Mr Mudge for the tiniest things. Now it would be Kevin's turn.

As Mr Mudge showed Mrs Trundle out, Tay Tui wandered over to Davey's table. She pulled out the chair Bella had vacated, sat down and plonked her backpack on the desk.

Davey noticed Tay's bag had stuff written all over it, things like 'I♥B4U' and 'B4U4ME'.

Humming to herself, Tay unzipped her bag and took out her pencil case. It was covered in the same slogans.

The new girl was clearly a big fan of the boy band B4U, a band Davey and his friends couldn't stand on principle (the principle being that any band loved by so many girls must be bad).

Now Davey noticed that someone – probably Tay – had drawn portraits in blue pen of each of the B4U members on the pencil case. Davey tried to work out who was who, but the pictures didn't look much like Lochie, Wills, Finn and Zac, the four band members. (Davey kicked himself. *How do I even know their names?*)

Now he noticed that Tay was singing to herself. She wasn't too bad – but then he realised what she was singing. It was B4U's big hit, the one that had catapulted the band to the top of the charts, where they'd been ever since, denying proper, good bands a shot at fame. 'You're My One, My Baby' was the worst song Davey had ever heard. The trouble was, as soon as you heard it you couldn't stop singing it – for weeks. *Aargh*!

'Who said that?' Mudge peered around the room with piggy eyes.

'Warner did, Sir.' It was Mo.

Davey woke from his awful daydream with a start.

For once, Mr Mudge let it go through to the keeper. He glared at Davey for a moment before continuing. 'As I was saying, class, I'm pleased to announce that one of 6M's students has been selected to perform at the town hall in the city as part of Senior Citizens' Week celebrations.'

Mr Mudge's lips parted, revealing a hint of yellow teeth. Davey guessed the teacher was attempting to smile kindly.

'As we all know, Kevin McNab is a ballroom dancer, which I must say is a far better use of your time' – Mudge looked across at Kevin and nodded approvingly – 'than playing cricket. Anyway, Kevin and his dance partner have been selected to perform with a troupe chosen from all over the city.'

Davey looked across at his friend and surreptitiously gave him the thumbs-up. Kevin rolled his eyes: he hated ballroom dancing, but his mum made him do it.

Mudge's ears glowed softly. 'So let's all give Kevin a clap and wish him luck for his performance this Friday. He should be very proud.'

6M burst into applause. But Davey sat there like a stunned toadfish. He looked across at Sunil, then Kevin, then George. They too were motionless, staring into space as if they'd been donged on the head by a fishmonger's mallet.

Davey was in such shock that even Tay Tui's singing couldn't stir him. Dylan's leaving had been bad enough. But now Kevin wouldn't be playing in the match on Friday either, and he was one of their best bats. How were Sandhill Flats going to even play against the Batfish, let alone *beat* them? It was too awful to contemplate.

And there was the new girl, Tay Tui, still singing, as if nothing was wrong.

'You know you need me, baby,
It's true, oo-oo-oo.'

Davey put his hands over his ears. *Aargh*!

'That was Warner again, Sir,' Mo said.

CHAPTER 3

NEW RECRUITS

Recess passed in a blur. At last the lunchtime bell rang. Finally, after a few false starts that caused Mr Mudge's ears to turn maroon, the teacher let the class out. Relieved, Davey grabbed his lunchbox and Kaboom, his special cricket bat made of English willow.

'At least we've got cricket training,'
Davey said to his friends as they crossed the
playground to their favourite lunch spot.

Sunil gave him a friendly push. 'Ready to
get behind the wicket? I know you love it.'

Davey groaned. He turned to Kevin.
'McNab, didn't you realise the dancing thing
was on the same day as the match?'

'No! I thought it wasn't on for ages.' Kevin
shrugged. 'Mum didn't tell me. But don't
worry, guys.' He sounded optimistic. 'I'll get
her to write a letter to the dance people. I'll
get out of it, no sweat.'

'You better.' George sounded glummer than
Davey, if that was possible.

Kevin grinned. 'Leave it to me!'

'Ah, boys! Lovely to see you arrive to training on time!' It was the nice new teacher, Ms Maro.

'What's she doing here?' Davey whispered to Sunil.

Sunil gave a little shrug that only Davey saw. 'Hi, Ms Maro,' he said, smiling so his dimple showed. 'Are you helping out today?'

Ms Maro grinned like she'd been handed a huge piece of ice-cream cake. 'I'm the new coach, Sunil.' She looked around at the gathering team members. 'In case you haven't noticed, I *love* cricket! So when Mrs Trundle was looking for a coach for the school team, I put up my hand.' She clapped in excitement. 'We are going to have *so* much fun!'

Davey's heart lifted just a tiny bit. Even though Ms Maro came across as entirely loopy, she actually *was* fun most of the time.

'Well, in that case . . . As captain, I'd like to welcome you, Ms Maro,' Sunil said, putting out his hand. 'But I guess we better get to it. We've got a big game on Friday.'

Davey knew what his friend was up to: if there was one thing the cricket players hated it was standing around talking when they could be having a hit, even if they were two players down.

Ms Maro smiled sunnily. 'We'll get started as soon as I've made a couple of announcements,' she said firmly.

She motioned for everyone to move closer. 'Now, first, as you know, Dylan has moved schools, so we need a new wicket-keeper.'

A look of sorrow crossed her face but was gone as quickly as it had arrived. 'Secondly, as you probably also know, clever Kevin here is dancing for our senior citizens on Friday, so won't be able to play. That means we're two players short.'

'No, it's okay, Ms Maro,' Kevin called out. 'My mum's going to write a letter.'

Ms Maro reached into her pocket. 'She's already done it, Kevin,' she said, waving a piece of paper. 'Mums are always ahead of the game, eh?' She smiled. 'Now, your mum says here –' Ms Maro held up the letter '– that you won't be coming to school at all that day, because you have to catch a bus to the town hall in the city and be there two hours before the performance at one o'clock.'

She looked over at Kevin. 'So, while we're hitting sixes and catching out Batfish, you'll be spinning your partner round the dancefloor for the senior citizens!'

She tucked the letter back in her pocket. 'Kevin, we're proud of you, but we're going to miss you on Friday, aren't we team?'

'Yes, Ms Maro,' the cricketers said in monotone unison.

Davey gave Kevin a push. 'Good one, McNab!' he hissed. 'Now what do we do?'

'So what we're hoping to do is . . .' Ms Maro looked around excitedly, as if they were all about to embark on a trip to the moon. 'We're *hoping* to enlist a couple of *new* players.'

'Great idea, Miss,' Sunil said, smiling so his dimple showed. 'But no one else knows how to play. We've tried it before.'

Davey nodded in agreement. 'It's true, Miss,' he said.

'Well, I think our luck's about to change,' Ms Maro said. 'Because I happen to know of two people who are *very* keen to join the team.'

Suddenly, Davey became aware of a sound he'd hoped never to hear again, the sound of that awful B4U song.

Ms Maro gestured to someone behind him. 'Come on, guys, come forward so we can all meet you!'

The cricket team took a step back to clear a path, and the two new potential recruits made their way to the front.

Davey sucked in a breath. He heard George hiss 'Oh no!' and Kevin turned and glared at him in horror. Then Davey's eyes locked on Sunil. The team captain was as pale as a freshly minted zombie.

'Has everyone met Tay Tui?' Ms Maro put her arm around the new girl's shoulder. 'Tay loves cricket and can't wait to try out for the team.'

The teacher's eyes sparkled. 'Of course, everyone knows our other candidate. He's better known for his skill on the footy field but he tells me he *loves* cricket as much! I wouldn't be surprised if he turns out to be the next Ricky Ponting!' Ms Maro put her arm around the other potential cricketer.

It was Mo.

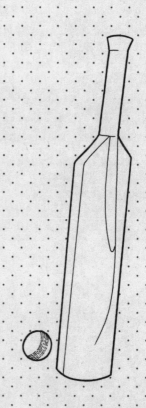

CHAPTER 4
KEEP IT DOWN!

Ms Maro wasted no time trying out Tay and Mo for the Sandhill Flats school cricket team.

Usually, the cricketers would have been glad to be out on the field playing, but this time their efforts looked half-hearted at best. Not that anyone was too bothered about Tay Tui trying out. After all, she was nice enough and if she could play cricket, well, it'd be good to have her on board. No, nearly everyone seemed happy for Tay to try out – everyone except Davey, who had already heard enough of Tay's singing to last a lifetime. It wasn't really the singing he couldn't stand, but what she sang – that awful, stupid, mindless and gross 'You're My One, My Baby'. Really, who could listen to that song once, let alone 900 times?

Ivy Mundine seemed particularly pleased that another girl might join the team. But when it came to Mo, the cricketers would have voted as one, if they'd been asked: everyone would have been opposed.

It wasn't because they didn't like Mo, although nobody *did* like Mo, mainly because *he* didn't like anyone much, especially cricketers. It was because everyone knew, especially Davey, Sunil, George and Kevin, that Mo *hated* cricket more than anything else in the world. So the cricketers were asking: *Why?* And because Mo was always making things up and couldn't, as far as anyone could tell, be trusted, it was a triple: *Why? Why? Why?*

But Ms Maro appeared to be oblivious to the problem, which was why she'd promptly organised for the two potential recruits to show off their stuff.

Tay Tui, it turned out, had played wicket-keeper at her previous school. It was her favourite position, she said. So she donned the gloves and took her place behind the stumps.

'Davey, you bat!' Ms Maro called. 'George, can you bowl?'

The boys nodded and took their positions.

Ms Maro clapped her hands. 'Okay, guys, let's do it!'

George walked back to his mark, then turned and stopped for a moment, looking at Davey.

Davey eyed him back. He was standing at the crease, tapping his bat, Kaboom, on the pitch. But all he could hear was:

'You know you need me, baby,
It's true, oo-oo-oo.'

Tay was at it again, singing that stupid song. Davey couldn't think, let alone concentrate.

George ran in and bowled an inswinger. Davey, unable to get the dumb song out of his head, misjudged it. The ball caught the edge of Kaboom and whizzed behind him.

'Out!' For once, Tay had stopped singing. Davey looked around. She was holding the ball aloft in her glove. 'Out!' she called again.

Ms Maro clapped. 'Well done, Tay! That was fantastic!' She looked at Davey. 'Tay's pretty good, eh, Davey? But is she good enough for the Sandhill Flats school team?'

Davey looked at Ms Maro. She really was a nice teacher, and she did have lovely brown eyes, but sometimes he wished she was less ... enthusiastic.

'Yeah, she's okay.' He turned and trudged off the pitch.

Ms Maro asked George to bowl a few more, this time to Kevin, but it was pretty obvious that Tay had made the team.

Soon it was Mo's turn. 'I'll bat,' he said grinning and waving a cricket bat around like a butterfly net.

'Deep, make sure you put him in it,' Davey said under his breath to his best friend. 'We're depending on you.'

'Thanks, Warner. Nice to be needed.' Sunil flashed him a half-smile and strolled out to his bowling mark looking determined.

Mo stood at the crease with his feet wide apart and stuck his bat out in the air in front of him. He bounced around on the spot. 'Send it down, Deep!' he hollered, baring his teeth. 'You can't beat me!'

Keep it down, Clouter! Davey thought. Mo had no idea how to hold a cricket bat.

Sunil bowled a yorker. Mo swung wildly, but missed by a metre or so. The ball sailed through to Tay, who caught it with one glove. In a second, she'd returned it to Sunil.

Sunil bowled again, this time an off-cutter.

Again Mo missed.

'Yeah!' Davey whispered. With a bit of luck, Mo might not make the team. He looked at George and Kevin. Simultaneously, they all held up crossed fingers.

Sunil bowled another attempted yorker. This time Mo ran down the pitch and managed to get an edge to the ball before it

bounced. Unfortunately, he hit it straight onto the bowler's wicket, sending the bails flying.

Ms Maro clapped her hands again. 'A good effort, Mo!' she called. 'Now, gather round, everyone, and let's have a chat.'

When everyone was in earshot, Ms Maro launched into her coach speech. 'I think we've got two new players with a lot of potential!' she said. 'Tay's our new wicket-keeper and Mo is first reserve. A bit more practice, Mo, and you'll soon be a key member of the team.'

She smiled so widely, Davey thought her face might crack. 'Congratulations, Tay and Mo! You're now officially members of the Sandhill Flats Primary School cricket team! Well done!' She clapped for the hundredth time that day.

The cricket team clapped too, but everyone appeared to be going through the motions. The thought of having Mo on the team was more than any sane cricketer could bear.

'Now, one more thing before we get back to training. This is serious . . .' Ms Maro suddenly looked so sad Davey felt like he should give her a hug.

'We've had a complaint . . . Someone – I don't know who – apparently said something unkind to the Batfish last time we played them.' Ms Maro glanced around. Davey thought her gaze lingered on him longer than the others.

'Now, as I'm sure you're all aware, at Sandhill Flats we play fairly, and putting the opposition off their game just isn't cricket.'

Ms Maro looked again at Davey, but he had no idea why. After all, Sunil was the one who had a way with words. Davey could never have even thought of half the things Sunil came up with. Like 'You smell like a fart in a firestorm' and 'Your sister chews cockroaches for fun'.

Ms Maro was still talking. 'The bottom line is, if any one of you says anything to put the Batfish off their game, we forfeit the match.' The teacher pursed her lips. 'Is that clear?'

Davey glanced at Sunil.

'Absolutely clear, Miss,' Sunil said. 'I don't know who was responsible last time, but it will never happen again while I'm captain.'

'Well, in that case, let's get to work!' Ms Maro handed a bat to Mo. 'Here you go.' She looked at Davey and smiled so her brown eyes sparkled. 'Davey, can you show Mo how to stand and give him a few tips?' She clapped her hands for the five-hundredth time that day. 'We're going to have so much fun! Watch out, Batfish!'

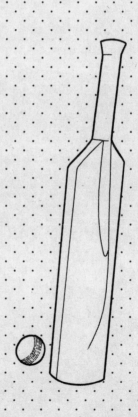

CHAPTER 5

A CRICKET CATASTROPHE

At lunchtime the next day, the Sandhill
Flats school cricket team dawdled down
to C playground for another training
session.

Usually Davey and his friends looked
forward to training so much they'd count

down the minutes. This time, however, they'd have preferred to be anywhere else.

For one thing, they missed Dylan. On the upside, they'd at least now heard from their friend, who had skyped George the night before and told him about his trip north, and how he'd seen the Big Banana and the Big Pineapple.

Also on the upside was the fact that everyone agreed Tay Tui might turn out to be an okay wicket-keeper – everyone, that is, except Davey, who still found Tay's singing and that stupid B4U song annoying.

But the boys were *extremely* disappointed that Kevin couldn't play on Friday against the Batfish, an unfortunate situation that had turned into a full-blown nightmare now Mo Clouter was in the team. Davey and his friends were unanimous about that – inviting Mo to join the team was like inviting a boa constrictor to a bandicoots' picnic. There could only be one outcome – and it wouldn't be pretty.

So, when they arrived at C playground to find Mo at the crease, swatting at balls like they were flies and yelling 'Not fair!' and 'You're toast!' every time he missed, Davey and his friends nearly turned around and trudged back to the classroom to spend the forty minutes with Mr Mudge. Anything had to be better than this.

At least Tay Tui was friendly, abandoning her post behind the wicket to offer everyone Whopper Chomp lollies from an open packet. 'I've never had these before!' she said, smiling widely. 'They're the best!'

Davey and his friends each took a sweet and nodded knowingly. Whopper Chomps were their favourite.

'Tay's all right,' Sunil said quietly in his captain's voice to Davey as he took the last sweet in the packet. 'She's in.'

Yeah, if she'd stop singing for a minute, Davey thought.

Ms Maro rushed over. 'Here you are!' she exclaimed joyfully, as if they were Santa's elves bearing gifts. 'Now, Davey, you can be the other batter. Sunil, you have a turn bowling. You other two can practise fielding in slips.'

Davey plodded to the bowler's end, dragging Kaboom behind him. He'd never felt so uninspired on a cricket pitch before.

Sunil paced out his run-up, then turned to face his nemesis. At least now Mo had his bat on the ground, but his feet were still wide apart, as if he was holding a golf club, and he was still bouncing on the spot.

Sunil ran in and bowled a full-length fast ball down the leg side. Mo ran out to meet it, trying to get his bat to it before it bounced. He missed and Tay Tui caught it and stumped him faster than Davey could say 'Ha!'

'Out!' Tay called.

'No' fair! Gi's another one! I'll smash it!' Mo was waving his bat threateningly in Sunil's direction.

Ms Maro stepped in. 'Okay, Mo, try again.' She turned to Sunil. 'Captain, we need to help our new recruit get up to speed. Bowl a little slower till Mo gets the hang of it.'

Sunil didn't smile or nod; in fact, Davey was sure he saw his best friend grimace before turning to go back to his mark.

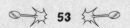

Ms Maro glanced at her watch. 'Now guys, I have to pop down to the office for ten minutes. Keep it up and I'll be back before you can say "Six!"' She gave a tinkly laugh, then set off at a jog across the playground.

For once Sunil did as he was told, and bowled a slower ball. Mo managed to hit it and ran down the pitch. Davey ran too, but had to sidestep Mo, who had begun zigzagging in front of him.

'Move over, Shorty!' Mo laughed.

Now at the crease and waiting to bat, Davey tried to put Mo out of his mind, even though his batting partner was grinning like a pufferfish at the bowler's end.

He breathed deeply and tried to focus. *Eye on the ball. Eye on the ball . . .*

'You're my one, my only, b-a-a-a-b-y-y-y,
It's no fun, I'm so lonely, b-a-a-a-a-a-a-a-a-a-
b-b-b-b-y-y-y-y-y.'

Tay was singing that stupid song again.

Aargh!

Sunil ran in and bowled a bouncer
down the leg side. Davey thought he'd try
his switch hit. He swapped the position
of his hands and turned. But his timing
was all wrong and in a split second the
ball was in Tay's gloves. Davey had to admit
she was pretty good.

'Close!' she said, flashing him a smile.

'She'll catch you next time!' Mo called from
the other end of the pitch.

Davey bit his tongue and gave him a friendly wave.

'If you care, if you care at all,
Just pick up your phone and make that call . . .'

Davey turned. 'Hey Tay, keep it down!' he said in a friendly tone.

'What?' Tay looked confused. 'I didn't say anything.'

'You were singing.'

'Was I? Oh, sorry.' Tay shook her head as if she'd just woken from a deep sleep.

Davey tapped the pitch lightly with Kaboom and tried to focus again. *Take a deep breath. Eye on the ball . . .*

Sunil ran in. Just as he reached the bowler's crease, Mo hooted loudly.

The noise took Sunil by surprise, and his ball went wide.

Davey let it go through to Tay.

'Ha! Those Batfish are gonna win by a mile!' Mo laughed.

'Clouter, you're on the team now,' Davey called out. 'You're one of *us*!'

Mo laughed again, and did a little shake and a wriggle. 'Maybe – or maybe not!'

Davey groaned.

'Shania said Mo was a bit thick.'

Davey turned.

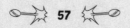

Tay was grinning at him. 'But I kind of like him.'

Davey raised an eyebrow. 'That makes two – you and his mum.'

'He reminds me of Zac. You know, the tall one in B4U?' Tay stared into the middle distance, as if she'd been hypnotised. 'He's got those dark eyes.'

'Eeewww!'

Tay shrugged and smiled to herself. '*You're my one –*'

'"*MY ONLY BABY*"! I *know!*' Davey had just about had enough. And it was only Tuesday.

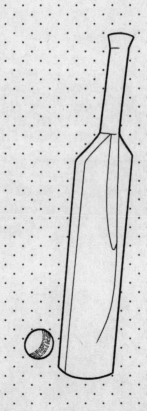

CHAPTER 6

CLEAN BOWLED AND OUT

The big match against Batfish Beach Primary was only two days away and things weren't exactly going smoothly for the Sandhill Flats team. Tay Tui had proved to be a more than able wicket-keeper and replacement for Dylan, but Mo Clouter was nothing short of a disaster as a temporary fill-in for Kevin.

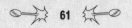

Everyone knew Mo hated cricket, so why he'd volunteered to join the school team was a mystery.

'He's up to something,' Davey said to Sunil as they dawdled into class on Wednesday morning.

'Yeah, and we need to find out what.'

'Deep, no more talk, unless it's about HSIE,' Mr Mudge barked.

Davey noticed that Mudge's ears already had a blood-orange tinge. However, the lesson started out reasonably well. Mudge droned on about the discovery of gold in Australia. Davey tried to listen – especially because George had said there was gold in the swamp at Flatter Park, and Davey thought Mr Mudge might get around to telling them how to find it. But soon the familiar sound of a certain

B4U song buzzed in his ear like a mosquito.
Tay was at it again.

'. . . *pick up your phone and make that call* . . .'

Davey tried to keep his eyes to the front.
He figured that if he didn't look at Tay he'd
have less chance of focusing on what she was
singing. But it didn't work. For some reason,
as soon as he heard the song he couldn't hear
anything else.

He glanced in Tay's direction. She was in
a trance again, staring into the middle
distance as she sang. Davey noticed that
on the desk in front of her was a Whopper
Chomp packet.

Oh-oh, he thought. He'd seen this before.
Mo Clouter had found a Whopper Chomp
packet on his desk not so long ago and it had
turned into a huge to-do because Sunil had

hidden rotten egg gas in it. Mudge's ears had stayed purple for days.

'*. . . you're my on-ly, ba-a-a-a-b-b-b-y-y-y . . .*'

Tay's hand reached absent-mindedly for the Whopper Chomp packet. She extracted a lolly and popped it in her mouth. The singing stopped.

But it was too late. 'Who's making that noise during HSIE?' Mudge's ears were tearing through the colours of the spectrum at the speed of sound. Davey couldn't take his eyes off them.

'Is that supposed to be singing? Whoever it is, don't think you're being funny.' The teacher looked around accusingly.

Mo put up his hand. 'It was Warner, Sir, singing that B4U song. He can't stop thinking about them.'

Mudge's cold gaze settled on Davey, his ears now violet.

Davey looked down at the desk in front of him. There, on top of his book, was Tay's Whopper Chomp packet. Someone – Mo – had pushed it there.

Mudge marched over and bent down so close that Davey could see bristles peeking out of his nostrils.

'Wa-a-a-a-r-ner!' Mr Mudge grabbed the lolly packet. 'What is this?'

'Not sure, Sir,' Davey mumbled. 'It's not mine.' He didn't say whose it was. He wasn't a <u>snitch</u>.

'They're Warner's, Sir.' It was Mo.

Mudge's ears had turned black. 'Is that correct, Warner?'

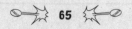

Davey looked at Tay Tui. She'd turned blue and her face had frozen in fear. He couldn't tell on her. 'Um, I don't know, Sir.'

'So while I'm out here doing my darnedest to fill that empty head of yours with at least a smidgeon of knowledge' – Mudge held up his thumb and forefinger to show how little knowledge he expected Davey to absorb – 'you're having a fine old time lazing around, singing songs and eating lollies. Is that right?'

'No, Mr Mudge.'

'Last time I found a packet of lollies on this table I recall that you were partly responsible.' Mudge turned to survey the class. 'And I promised you all then that if I *ever* found someone eating lollies again in class, I'd make an example of that person.'

'Yes, Mr Mudge.'

'Warner, I'm determined to teach you something, if it's the last thing I do.' Now Mudge's whole head was purple. It looked like a giant eggplant with hair. 'That's it. Instead of playing sport on Friday you can help me polish the lawn bowls. And if there's any time left over, I'm sure Mrs Trundle will be able to put you to good use.'

Mudge bared his teeth in an evil grin. 'So that means you'll miss the cricket match this week. You're going to have to learn the hard way.'

'Mr Mudge?' Tay had her hand up. 'I . . .'

Mudge shook his head sadly. 'Tay, no doubt you're feeling sorry for Warner, but he deserves everything he gets. He'll never learn, otherwise. So I don't want to hear any more about it.'

He peered around the room. 'I'm sure someone else could take Warner's place in Friday's game. Any volunteers?'

Bella Ferosi's hand shot up. 'I'm an excellent cricketer, Mr Mudge,' she said. 'I've never joined the cricket team because I'm the netball captain, as everyone knows.' She looked around the room, searching for confirmation. 'But we have a bye in netball this week, so I'd be happy to captain the cricket team.'

Grinning maliciously, Mudge looked across at Sunil. 'Well, I'll suggest that to Ms Maro,' he said. 'I'm sure she'd be happy to give you a turn as cricket captain, Bella. It's good to allow others the opportunity to shine, don't you agree, Deep?'

Davey eyed Sunil. His friend had that zombie look again. Sunil was proud to be captain of both the school team and their club team, the Sandhill Sluggers, and he had every right to be – he was a great captain, even if he did sometimes let slip the odd word or two to the other side.

Bella, on the other hand, was the bossiest person Davey had ever met. A cricket team with Bella and Mo in it was a team Davey would never want to join. He shook his head in despair.

'Don't worry, Shorty,' Mo whispered. 'I'll take care of those Batfish.' He giggled. 'You can count on me.'

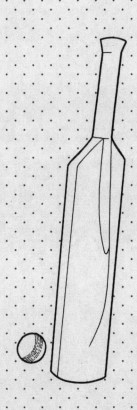

CHAPTER 7

TRAINING TRAUMA

'Just because you can't play doesn't mean
you can't come to training.' Sunil had his
arm around Davey's shoulder as they
rounded the toilet block and headed across
C playground.

'Yeah, same as me,' Kevin said. 'I'm still going to training. It's better than sitting around doing nothing.'

They reached the cricket pitch. Some of the team were already there, but Ms Maro was yet to arrive.

'What about Bella?' Davey was in a funk. 'They can't make her captain!'

'Nah, that'll never happen.' Sunil sounded his usual happy self. 'I'll eat Mo's stinky hat if they make Bella captain.'

Davey was about to make Sunil shake on it – bets like these always cheered him up – when someone called out his name.

'Davey!'

He turned. Tay Tui was running towards them with Ivy Mundine close behind.

'I'm so sorry, bro!' Tay was panting. 'I tried to tell Mr Mudge again just now, but he still wouldn't listen. It was like he didn't really want to know . . .'

'He didn't. He's always like that.' Ivy frowned. 'It's bad luck, though. And now look who's coming.' She pointed.

They turned to see. Bella had just rounded the toilet block and was striding towards them. She was carrying a bat. When she saw them staring, she waved. 'Hi, everyone! You ready to get stuck in?'

'Don't tell me . . .' This time Sunil looked as if a vampire had drained his whole body of blood. Even the tips of his hair looked grey.

Bella paused to catch her breath, then put one hand on her hip. 'So, I'm thinking we'll start with some warm-ups, then we'll do ten laps of the playground. Then I'll practise my bowling while Tay and George bat. Sunil, you'll be wicket-keeper –'

'Um . . .'

Davey had never seen Sunil at a loss for words. There was always going to be a first time, though.

'Um . . . Um . . . Ah . . .'

'So, let's start with some stretches.' Bella dropped the bat she was holding. 'Everyone space out and do what I do.' She stood with her feet apart, took a deep breath and raised her arms.

No one moved. She stopped to look around.

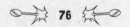

Davey glanced at Sunil and stifled a laugh. The situation was so desperate it was funny. Sunil tried not to smile.

'Come on, guys! Let's get to it!' Bella reached up high then swung low, turning as she went, so her fingertips brushed her toes. She reversed the action. 'Now the other way. Davey? Sunil? Ivy?'

Still no one budged.

'Good to see you guys have started already! Well done!' Ms Maro was rushing towards them. The rest of the team were running behind, carrying the gear.

Bella turned. 'Ah, Ms Maro, you've made it at last.' She waited for the teacher and the other kids to reach them.

'Ms Maro, since I'm captain this week, I'd be happy to run the training. I'm a very good leader.' Bella smiled, then turned back to the cricketers, who now stood with their arms crossed.

'Thanks. That's a lovely offer.' Ms Maro smiled and patted the school captain on the back. 'But Sunil Deep is already team captain.'

'Mr Mudge said I could be!' Bella suddenly sounded like a four-year-old who'd been told Christmas was cancelled. 'He said it was time to give someone else an opportunity to shine – which I happen to be good at.' She gave her ponytail a flick. 'Shining, I mean.'

Ms Maro put her arm around Bella's shoulder, a look of sympathy on her face. 'Yes, I talked to Mr Mudge about that, and we agreed that perhaps this week was not the right week to change captain. If you'd like to join the team, that's great, but Sunil's our captain, isn't he, guys?'

'Yeah!' everyone shouted, punching the air in relief.

'No!' It was Mo. He'd sneaked up behind them.

'Mo, you've always got a funny line to keep us laughing!' Ms Maro shook her head in amusement. 'Now, let's get to it!'

Bella put her hands on her hips and frowned. 'I only joined on the condition that I be captain. I need to *lead*, Ms Maro, not *follow*.'

'Sorry, Bella,' Ms Maro said firmly. 'But I have to put the team first, and on this occasion that means keeping things as they are.'

Bella flicked her ponytail so hard Davey thought it might fly off. 'In that case, I'd better go. I have important duties to attend to.' With that, the school captain marched off across the playground.

'Looks like Bella won't be playing after all,' Sunil said quietly to Davey. 'Shame.'

'Yeah. Oh well . . .' Davey had to admit Ms Maro was a lot cleverer than she looked.

Ms Maro clapped her hands. 'So, let's get started.'

She looked over at Tay. The new girl had pulled a packet of Whopper Chomps out of her pocket and was about to extract a lolly from it. 'Tay, no lollies while we're training.'

Tay looked up in surprise. 'Sorry, Miss,' she said. She glanced at Ivy Mundine, who was standing right beside her. It seemed the two girls had become friends.

'*You're my one, my on-l-y-y-y-y-y . . .*' Tay sang.

'*B-a-a-a-b-y-y-y-y*,' Ivy sang in response. The girls burst out laughing.

Oh no, thought Davey. Now Tay had Ivy doing it. Where would it end?

Ms Maro frowned. 'Save your singing for choir, girls.' She turned to look at Davey. 'Mr Warner, I hear you won't be playing on Friday? That's a shame.'

'Yeah, Mr Mudge said I was singing in class and eating Whopper Chomps, Miss. But can I still train?'

'Of course, Davey.' Ms Maro glanced at Tay and Ivy. The two girls had finished their Whopper Chomps and singing and were busy setting up the wickets. 'And I might have a word to Mr Mudge.' She smiled. 'Now, Davey, grab Kaboom. You and George can bat first.'

Ms Maro wasn't half as kooky as she first appeared. In fact, Davey would have gone so far as to call her the best teacher he'd ever met. Not that she had much competition, now that he thought about it.

He ran over and grabbed Kaboom. He wasn't going to let anyone or anything stop him from playing the Batfish on Friday.

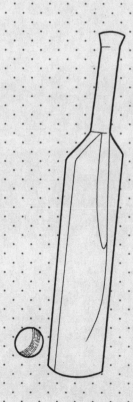

CHAPTER 8

TALKIN' TANGO

With Bella off to attend to her 'important duties' and Mo under Ms Maro's surveillance, training *should* have been fun. But despite repeated requests from the teacher, Tay continued to sing behind the wicket. She didn't even know she was doing it, Davey realised now, which made it all the more difficult to get her to stop. And once more it put Davey off his game.

And even though Ms Maro kept a close eye on Mo, the clueless cabbage still managed to wind up the entire team. One thing in particular that Mo said was so disturbing that Davey was forced to call an emergency after-school meeting of his three best friends.

He'd been standing at the crease, Kaboom in hand. Behind him, Mo was having a turn as wicket-keeper.

While Davey waited for George to bowl, and with Ms Maro well out of earshot, Mo kept up a constant stream of annoying talk. Most of it didn't even make any sense. But it was the next thing that Mo said that got Davey really worried. 'I'm gonna make sure those Batfish win on Friday, Shorty. Shouldn't be too hard.'

Davey turned around to eye Mo. There was never any point replying when Mo was fired up. And if he kept quiet, Mo would let slip what he was up to.

Mo went on, his chest puffing with pride. 'All I need to do is keep talking to their bowler on the field, let him know what I think of his style. And their fielders, and their wicket-keeper. That should do it.' Mo smirked like a sick toad. 'The Batfish'll thank me after.'

So as soon as training had finished, Davey called the meeting for after school. For convenience, it was held at the corner shop, which belonged to Benny, the Sandhill Sluggers' coach, and his wife, Barb.

'So what's all this about, Warner?' Sunil looked serious.

'Clouter's planning to put the Batfish off their play so we forfeit the game.'

'How do you know?' Kevin looked sceptical.

'He told me. He's going to say things to them when they're fielding.'

'Well, that's it,' Sunil said firmly. 'We've got to get him out of the team.'

'And while we're at it, can we do something about Tay Tui?' Davey knew Tay was good behind the wicket, but something had to be done.

'What do you mean?' Sunil looked confused. 'She's pretty good. And she likes Whopper Chomps, which is handy.'

'Yeah, but she sings all day. That horrible B4U song. It's driving me mad!'

The other three boys shook their heads. 'Yeah, that song really sucks,' George said.

'It's a shocker.' Kevin sighed.

'Sure is.' Sunil looked thoughtful for a moment. He snapped his fingers. 'Got it! Tay can't sing if she's sucking a Whopper Chomp. So we load her up with them every time we play.' He looked around at his friends. 'We'll have to pool our money for this. Do it for the team, okay?'

They all nodded. It was such a simple but clever plan. Sunil really was a genius, Davey decided.

'But what about Clouter?' Davey knew this wasn't going to be an easy one.

Sunil snapped his fingers again. 'Easy! We send him to another cricket ground. We'll just tell him it's over at Shimmer Bay Park. By the time he finds out, we'll have finished the game.' Sunil smiled and tapped his head.

'Mmmm, not sure,' Kevin said.

'Why?' George asked. 'Sounds like a good plan to me.'

'No, it won't work,' Davey said. 'Ms Maro's already told us it's a home Batfish game, so Clouter will smell a rat if we tell him it's changed.'

Sunil's smile faded. He shrugged. 'Yeah, maybe you're right. But we've got to do something. In the meantime, everyone needs to put in money so we can buy a shedload of Whopper Chomps for Tay. Now!'

The boys all made a show of emptying their pockets. Sunil waited, his arms folded, until they'd coughed up everything they had. Then he added it all up on the counter.

Benny watched from behind his newspaper. 'You boys having a party?' he said when Sunil pushed the pile of coins towards him.

'Nah, someone else will be, though. Give us six packs of Whopper Chomps please, Benny. That should do it.'

Davey watched as the money changed hands and Sunil pocketed the lolly packets. 'Don't go sampling them, Deep,' he said. 'We're going to need every single one of those.'

Sunil smiled so his dimple showed. 'You can trust me. Now, what about Clouter?'

'We could tell Ms Maro what he said.' George looked uncertain. It wasn't a solution any of them would usually consider. 'Never tell, never worry,' was their motto.

The other boys shook their heads. Even though Mo was a pugnacious pest, they wouldn't go so far as to tell on him.

'No point dragging in teachers. Takes all the fun out of it.' Sunil grimaced.

'I think we just have to make sure McNab and Warner play,' George said. 'Clouter's only a reserve. So if they can play, he'll have to sit out.'

'But couldn't he call out from the sidelines?' Now Kevin was doing the thinking.

Davey shook his head. 'He'll be sitting next to Ms Maro. He won't be able to.'

Sunil looked around at his friends. 'So tonight, we all need to come up with a plan to make sure McNab gets out of the dance thing and Mudge lets Warner play. How hard can it be?'

Everyone shook hands. But later, as Davey rode home on his old bike, with Max trotting along beside him, he couldn't help thinking it could be very hard indeed. Kevin's mum was dead keen on him dancing, and she was no pushover. And as for Mr Mudge . . .

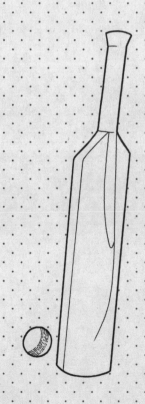

CHAPTER 9

MARO MAGIC

Davey left for school early the next day.
As soon as he arrived, he headed for
Ms Maro's classroom, where she could be
found most mornings, getting things ready
for the first lesson. He knocked on the
open door.

Ms Maro was at her desk, marking work. She looked up and smiled. 'Mr Warner! What brings you here?'

Davey took a few tentative steps into the classroom. 'I – I – I was wondering whether you ended up talking to Mr Mudge.'

The teacher put her head on one side and raised her eyebrows in question.

'About whether I can play against the Batfish tomorrow,' Davey explained. 'You see, I wasn't singing or eating lollies in class. It wasn't me.'

'Ah!' Ms Maro nodded knowingly. 'I'm sure it wasn't. I haven't spoken to Mr Mudge yet, but I will, right now.'

She got to her feet and smiled as if she'd just seen a rainbow. 'Mr Mudge isn't really mean, you know, Davey. I'm sure I can talk him around.'

I'm sure you can, Davey thought. Somehow, Ms Maro seemed to always get her way. If anyone could help him get back in the team for Friday's game against the Batfish, it was her.

With his mission accomplished, Davey headed down to C playground, where Sunil and the others were already playing cricket. Tay was behind the wicket, Sunil was at the crease and George was bowling. Ivy was also at the bowler's end, bat in hand.

George bowled. Sunil moved forward down the pitch but his bat didn't connect with the ball. A split second later, Tay had stumped him.

'Out, Deep!' Davey yelled.

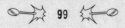

Sunil stopped in his tracks, turned and gave the new wicket-keeper a little clap. 'You're good, Tui, really good,' he said, nodding. He looked over at Davey. 'Warner, you have a turn. But watch out for Tay!'

Davey pulled Kaboom out of his backpack. He wandered over and took his position at the crease. *Here we go*, he thought. *She'll start singing that awful song any minute.*

But there was silence. Davey glanced behind him. Tay was in position, but her cheeks were bulging like a bullfrog's.

'How's it going?' Davey said as a test.

Tay nodded and made a loud sucking noise.

Davey smiled. 'So you like those Whopper Chomps?'

Tay nodded again and gave him the thumbs-up. She grinned. Her mouth was chock-full of lollies.

She wouldn't be doing any singing for a while, Davey decided. It solved that problem, at least temporarily. Now Davey and his friends had to work on making sure he and Kevin played in Friday's match.

'Ready, Warner?' George was standing at his mark, waiting to bowl.

Davey tapped Kaboom on the ground. 'You bet!'

For the first time all week, Davey got to bat in peace, and managed to pull off some nice shots. But soon the school bell sounded and the cricketers had to pull up stumps.

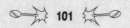

'So, any ideas about how we can get Warner and McNab back in the team for tomorrow?' Sunil asked as they strolled across the playground to class.

'Yeah, I know what I'm going to do.' Davey glanced at his friend – he knew Sunil wouldn't like his plan.

'What?'

'I'm going to beg for mercy,' Davey said. 'I've already asked Ms Maro to put in a good word for me. Now I'm going to offer to polish Mudge's lawn bowls and help out Mrs Trundle.'

Sunil frowned. 'That's a lame idea, Warner. Not very imaginative.'

'Maybe, but it's all I could come up with.'

Sunil looked disappointed. 'Okay, give it a try.' He glanced around at the others. 'What about McNab? Any thoughts?'

'I've got a few.' George looked confident. 'Kevin could let off the fire alarm at the town hall so they have to evacuate.'

Sunil shook his head. 'But he wouldn't get back quickly enough.'

'I could sneak off early, before we leave to catch the bus, and then turn up to the match in disguise.' Judging from his face, even Kevin knew it wouldn't work.

Sunil looked unimpressed. 'Next!'

'Okay, I've got one.' George sounded confident.

'Yeah? What?' Everyone was all ears.

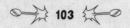

George was about to explain when they rounded the corner of the toilet block and bumped into Mr Mudge.

'Warner, Ms Maro tells me you've offered to do a few jobs around the school today in return for permission to play in the match against Batfish Beach tomorrow.' Judging by the colour of his ears, for once the teacher wasn't irate.

Davey nodded. 'Yes, Sir. Anything you like.'

George and Kevin gave him a pat on the back.

'Excellent.' Mr Mudge crossed his arms. 'So, at recess, you can polish the lawn bowls. At lunch, report to Mrs Trundle. There are quite a few things that need doing around her office. I'm sure she'll find a use for you.'

'No problem, Mr Mudge.'

Mr Mudge waved them past. 'Now, straight to class.'

They set off again, moving quickly this time, with Mudge bringing up the rear.

'Good one, Warner,' Sunil whispered in Davey's ear as they approached the classroom. 'What a crazy idea! Who'd have thought you'd pull it off?'

Davey rolled his eyes. 'Thanks for the vote of confidence, Deep.'

'Now, we've just got to get McNab out of his dancing thing,' Sunil muttered. 'Wonder what Pepi's other idea was?'

CHAPTER 10

GEORGE'S NO-BRAINER

Davey spent all of recess in the sports storeroom polishing the school's lawn bowls.

Mr Mudge, who loved lawn bowls almost as much as he hated cricket, was on hand to supervise. 'Like this, Warner,' he said, carefully picking up one of the bowls as if it was a brand-new puppy. He dipped a rag into a bucket of warm soapy water. 'Gently rub it in circles. Then use another rag to dry.'

For once, Davey made a real effort to do exactly what his teacher asked.

'Once it's dry, you give it a quick spray with the polish, and then another good rub until it shines. Got it?'

Davey nodded and eyed the six sets of bowls that Mr Mudge had lined up. It would take all recess and lunchtime to get it done.

Mr Mudge seemed to read his mind. 'These will keep you busy for a while. So you'll have to help Mrs Trundle *after* school.'

Davey nodded. Whatever Mrs Trundle had lined up for him, he figured it would be worth it if it meant he could play in the match the next day.

But at the end of the school day, when he was standing in Mrs Trundle's office, his optimism evaporated.

'I have just the job for a boy like you.' Mrs Trundle's eye twitched as she led him towards the big cupboard in the corner.

She pulled open the cupboard doors to reveal the shelves within. They were stacked with all kinds of stationery – scissors and glue, rulers and erasers, protractors and pins, boxes of bulldog clips.

The centre shelves were stacked closely together. Now Mrs Trundle pulled one of them towards her, like a drawer. Davey leaned forward to see what was on it.

Paperclips. Thousands of them, all in little compartments.

Davey had heard the legend of Mrs Trundle's paperclip collection, but no one had ever actually seen it so Davey had never believed the stories were true. And yet here he was, staring at the collection, perhaps the first person in the world (other than Mrs Trundle) to ever set eyes on it.

'It's the biggest paperclip collection in the southern hemisphere,' Mrs Trundle said proudly. There are four shelves like this one. But, as you can see, they need some re-sorting. That's your job.'

Davey took a closer look. Even he had to admit that the paperclips were in some disarray, with big ones jumbled in with small ones, and blue ones with orange ones.

Mrs Trundle glanced up at the big clock on the wall. 'I'll be here until half past five. You have until then to get these in order.' She smiled. 'You might receive a merit award for this, David. Now, chop chop!'

By the time Davey climbed on his bike to ride home, he could hardly see from all the sizing and sorting and picking and positioning. When he reached his house, Sunil, George and Kevin were hitting a ball around on the footpath out the front.

Sunil stopped in the middle of his bowling run-up. 'How'd you go?'

'Done! I'm in!' Davey raised his fist in victory. 'Batfish, here I come!'

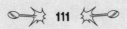

'Good one!' Sunil gave him a slap on the back.

George put his hand in his pocket and pulled out a Whopper Chomp. 'Here, Warner, a little reward.'

Davey popped the lolly into his mouth.

'We've got some other good news,' Sunil said. 'Pepi has come up with a good plan to get McNab out of dancing.'

'Yeah? What?'

'Well, I've been reading about tarantulas,' George said. 'Apparently, if one bites you it makes you dance like crazy and wave your arms about.'

'Mmm. And?' Davey couldn't see what any of this had to do with Kevin, but he was keen to find out.

'So the idea is, Kevin pretends he's been bitten by a tarantula and does a crazy dance, waving his arms around a lot. He won't be able to do the ballroom dancing because you have to hold your partner the whole time.'

Davey made a cross-eyed face. 'Doesn't that mean he'll miss the cricket too?'

'No. He just does it long enough to miss going to the dancing thing, and then gets better in time to play cricket. It's brilliant!' Sunil's eyes were shining with excitement.

'Wouldn't it be easier to pretend to be sick?' Davey asked.

'Nah, Mum won't fall for that,' Kevin said. 'But spiders! She hates them, so it'll freak her out. And Dad's away, so he won't know.'

'Of course, there aren't actually any tarantulas in Australia,' Sunil said knowledgeably. 'And it's true that a tarantula bite doesn't actually make you dance so much as twitch – and only *sometimes*. But, you've got to admit, it's brilliant, a no-brainer. Much better than yours, Warner.' Sunil grinned.

'Yeah, it's good,' Davey said. 'Do you need a big spider? Because I know where one lives. I might be able to catch it, so long as you don't hurt it.'

Kevin put his hand on his heart. 'Promise.'

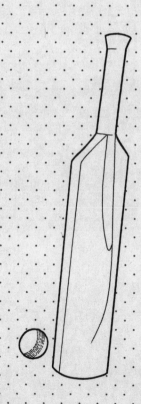

CHAPTER 11

'TARANTULA'

That night after dinner, Davey passed up a game of backyard cricket with his brother, Steve. 'Nah, I'm too tired,' he said, rubbing his eyes.

Davey's mum looked at him as if he'd turned into an alien. 'You? Tired? What've you been up to?'

'Nothing . . . But I need a jar with a lid. There's a spider on my wall and I need to catch him to put him outside.'

After a lot of rattling around in the back of a cupboard, Davey's mum found an old Vegemite jar. 'Careful not to drop it,' she said. 'And make sure you let him out as far away as possible. *I hate spiders.*'

Armed with the jar and broom, Davey and his dog Max headed for Davey's bedroom. The spider Davey was after often hid behind the poster of Ricky Ponting that hung on his bedroom wall.

After punching a few holes in the jar lid with a pen nib, Davey climbed onto his bed and carefully tugged on the corner of the poster. 'Whoops,' he whispered. The sticky stuff on the back of the corner had come off the wall, bringing a big chunk of

paint with it. 'Don't tell Mum,' he hissed
at Max.

Davey peered behind the poster, but it
was too dark to see. 'Max, get the torch!'
He pointed at the bedside table.

Max wagged his tail and barked before
dashing out through the door. Davey heard the
sound of his claws skittering down the hallway.

'Idiot pooch,' he muttered as he reached
down and grabbed the penlight. He switched
it on and shone it up behind Ricky. In the
upper corner, he spotted a dark shadowy
form. 'Gotcha!'

Except he hadn't, not yet. He grabbed the
broom and gently poked the end up behind
the poster. Nothing happened. He shone
the light up again – the spidery form hadn't
moved.

Max ran in and barked.

'We'll have to take Ricky down.' Davey
gently pulled the other bottom corner of the
poster off the wall. 'Ouch.' Another big chunk
of wall and paint came off. He reached up
and tugged carefully at a top corner – the
one he was fairly sure didn't hide a giant
spider. He looked down at Max, who was
standing on the bed next to him, his two
front paws up on the wall.

'Ready?' With the jar in one hand and
the broom in the other, Davey pulled on
the last corner. At the same time the poster
came away, a big brown spider scuttled down
the wall. Davey quickly stuck the broom in
front of it. The spider clambered on and in
a moment was running down the handle
towards him. Still holding the broom, Davey
held the jar at the end of handle. The spider
ran straight into it.

'The lid!' Davey slapped his hand over the top of the jar and cast his eyes around. There it was near the end of his bed. He dived and slammed it on.

'*Now* I've gotcha!'

After setting the jar on his bedside table, Davey rescued his poster of Ricky Ponting and stuck it up quickly, so his mum wouldn't see all the chunks out of the wall.

'So, what do you reckon, Ricky?' Davey stared into the former Australian captain's eyes. 'Will things work out tomorrow?'

Ricky's face looked like a huge green moon in the half-light of dusk. Davey threw himself back on the bed, and Max jumped on top of him.

'Get off!' Davey pushed the dog to the floor.

It had been a long day of polishing lawn bowls, sorting paperclips and catching spiders. Davey could hardly keep his eyes open. Still, he stared up at Ricky. 'Can we beat the Batfish, Ricky?' he whispered.

Did he see his hero wink? A thought came into his mind out of nowhere. Tay Tui was a good wicket-keeper – a *really* good one. If she also liked to sing, well, he'd have to get used to that.

But what about Mo?!

Davey knew what his mum would say. *'Give him a chance! Maybe Mo will learn to love cricket.'*

'Hmmm.' Davey wasn't buying it. That was *never* going to happen.

He looked at his spider. 'We're counting on you,' he said.

The creature was playing dead, but Davey was sure he saw one of its legs move . . .

The next morning, Davey was up early. After a quick breakfast of Corn Pops, he grabbed everything needed for the big game and jumped on his bike.

Stuffed into his school backpack he had his cricket gear, his bat, Kaboom, his 'baggy green', and, importantly, the Vegemite jar with the spider in it.

'Max, you're staying here,' he said firmly as he closed the back door behind him. Davey's dog was not only banned from the school grounds but from any school sporting fixture in the district. Max was that famous.

Davey wheeled his bike down the side path, then jumped on and headed to Kevin's place to give him the spider.

He couldn't let his friend down. After all, it was going to be incredible. He could see his friend now, doing the tarantula dance and freaking out his mum.

Davey laughed out loud. Mrs McNab would fall for it for sure. He could feel it in his bones.

CHAPTER 12

SANDHILL FLATS SLUMP

Lessons dragged that Friday morning. Mr Mudge seemed to take forever to explain long division for the hundredth time. Then he droned on about healthy eating choices in PDHPE for an hour, before asking Bella Ferosi to make an impromptu speech about leadership. Finally, after what felt like thirty-seven hours, 6M was allowed out for lunch.

Davey, Sunil and George quickly made their way to the school gate to wait for the rest of the cricket team. The plan was to walk to Flatter Park around the corner, where the match would be played.

'No sign of McNab,' George observed as they strode towards the gate and freedom.

'We'll see him down at Flatter.' Sunil seemed confident. 'He's got to be sick and crazy enough to miss the dancing but get better quickly enough to make the match. It's a fine line, but I reckon he'll do it.'

Davey wanted to believe his friend, but now he wasn't so sure. For one thing, the spider had played dead for so long he wondered whether it was actually alive at all. In which case, would Kevin's mum fall for the trick? It was touch and go.

At the gate, Ms Maro was ticking names off a list. 'Ah, here they are! My star players!' She smiled at Davey and his friends, then looked up and over their heads. 'Oh, and here's Mo and Tay and Ivy! I didn't hear you coming!'

Davey glanced around. Tay, Ivy and Mo were a few steps behind them. But Ms Maro was right: the girls' mouths were so full of lollies, they couldn't make a sound.

'Hi, everyone!' Mo leered at Davey. 'Looking forward to losing?'

Davey gave the mini-minded muppet a happy smile.

When everyone was accounted for, the team formed two straggly lines and set off towards Flatter Park.

Two and a half minutes later, they were there. The Batfish Beach team had already arrived and had started warming up.

Davey scanned the field. Kevin was nowhere to be seen. 'McNab's not here,' he said quietly to Sunil.

'That's okay. If he comes any time before afternoon tea, they'll let him play.' Sunil still sounded confident.

'So long as Mo doesn't say anything to the Batfish before McNab gets here.'

'It's a risk we'll have to take.'

When it was time to toss the coin, Kevin still hadn't arrived. Sunil called tails, won, and opted to bat first.

'Hopefully McNab makes it by the time it's his turn to bat,' Sunil whispered as Davey pulled on his helmet and gloves. Then he'll be here to do some bowling when the Batfish are in.'

As he trudged out to the pitch with George, who was Sandhill Flats' other opening batsman, Davey scanned Flatter Drive. Still no sign of Kevin.

He took his place at the crease and tried to put Kevin, Mo and that awful B4U song out of his head for good. At this point, his main job was to take his time, score some runs and set Sandhill Flats up for a nice big run tally. He gave Kaboom a quick kiss for good luck. 'Come on, K, we can do this,' he whispered to his bat. Then he got into position and waited, ready.

The first Batfish bowler started with a few leg-spinners. Davey took it slow – so slow that by the end of the over he hadn't scored a run.

That's okay, he told himself. No rush. Then George at the other end also played out a maiden over.

After two overs with no runs to the score, Davey was pleased when, first ball next over, the bowler strayed down the leg side. Davey shifted his weight onto his back foot and pulled the ball to cow corner for three.

With George on strike, Davey watched as his friend blocked the first few balls. George was right to take it slow, he knew; but he was out LBW to the last ball of the over. He hadn't even had a chance to settle in.

Davey grimaced as George trudged off. One for three was not a great start.

Next up was Ivy. As she approached, Davey noticed she was no longer sucking on a lolly. He just hoped she wasn't going to start singing, like her new friend Tay.

But Ivy didn't sing – at least, Davey couldn't hear her. Instead she started scoring steadily with some stylish shots that had the Batfish fielders running everywhere.

It gave Davey the confidence to try a couple of his own scoring shots and forget about Kevin, Mo and B4U in the process. His score climbed to fourteen.

When Byron, the Batfish captain, sent a fast one down the leg side, Davey jumped at the chance to try his switch hit, something he'd been working on for ages.

With some fancy footwork, he turned, swapped hands on the bat handle, and played a right-handed drive for four valuable runs.

'Now we're getting somewhere!' Ivy called out from the other end of the pitch.

But a few balls later, Davey was out for twenty-one, caught in slips when Kaboom didn't quite connect.

Usually at this point, Kevin would have come in to bat. But as Davey traipsed back to the boundary his friend was still nowhere to be seen.

'Good one, Shorty,' Mo hissed as Davey passed. 'Wait till I get out there and start bothering those Batfish. Ha!' Mo's pink eyes were gleaming.

Ignoring the blithering blockhead, Davey eyed Sunil. 'No McNab?'

Sunil shook his head. 'Not yet. Tay's up instead.'

'Tay, no lollies out there,' Ms Maro said as the new girl pulled on her gloves. 'We don't want you to choke.'

'Sure, Miss,' Tay said before heading out to the pitch. 'I don't have any left, anyway.'

That's a worry, Davey thought. *Tay'll be singing for the rest of the match.* He made a note to ask to field on the boundary, as far as possible from the warbling wicket-keeper.

Davey had no idea whether Tay or Ivy were singing out on the pitch. But they certainly made some great shots and scored some quick

runs. When Tay did get out it was unlucky –
she stumbled going for a quick single and was
run out. Still, she had scored a respectable
sixteen runs.

Even without Kevin playing, it now looked
as if they'd reach a competitive total, but when
Ivy was dismissed for nineteen, it led to a
collapse. The rest of the Sandhill Flats batters
came and went with almost no runs added
to the score. Sunil, at his usual number ten
position in the batting order, added a few runs
to the tally before being caught behind.

The result was that, even though Ivy, Tay
and Davey had batted well and notched up
decent scores, Davey doubted it would be
enough. To have any chance of beating the
Batfish, Sandhill Flats would need at least
eighty-five runs or so. As it was, they were
sitting on sixty-nine. It would be up to their
last batter to bump up the score.

Unfortunately, with no sign of Kevin, the only batter left for Sandhill Flats was Mo Clouter.

Davey, George and Sunil exchanged worried looks. If Mo's performance at cricket training was anything to go by, his chances of scoring even one run were slim. On top of that, the cocky cabbage was no doubt hell-bent on pestering the Batfish. If that happened and he was caught, Sandhill Flats would be disqualified on the spot.

They watched as Mo grabbed a bat and started swatting invisible flies before tramping across the field towards the crease.

George shook his head. 'How did it come to this? I was sure our spider plan would work.'

'Yeah, me too,' Sunil said. 'It seemed like a no-brainer.'

Davey nodded. 'It did. Speaking of no-brainers, Mo's almost ready to go.'

They held their breath . . .

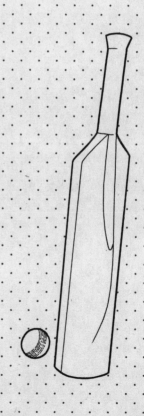

CHAPTER 13

THE WARBLING
WICKET-KEEPER

Davey watched as Mo planted his feet wide
apart and waved his bat around in the air.
'Keep the bat *down*! Didn't he learn anything
at training?'

'Not about cricket,' George said.

The bowler ran in and let the ball fly.

Mo ran forward, holding his bat as if he was playing ping pong. He swung at the ball, which sailed past him and straight into the wicket-keeper's gloves. Mo was halfway down the pitch as the wicket-keeper casually stumped him.

He was out for a golden duck.

The Batfish jumped for joy.

Mo turned and looked behind him, then threw his bat on the ground and stormed off.

Davey sighed loudly. 'Well, that's it, then. All out for sixty-nine. We're done like a dinner.'

'At least he didn't get a chance to say much out there,' Sunil said.

'He couldn't have anyway,' George said. 'Check him out.'

Now only metres away, they could see that his cheeks were bulging so much he really did look like a pufferfish.

'Whopper Chomps,' Sunil whispered.

'You're my one, my only-y-y-y-y –'

Davey turned. Tay was back at it. He groaned.

Ms Maro clapped her hands. 'Tay, quiet for a moment, please.' She smiled. 'Now, everyone, gather round.'

The players dragged themselves to their feet and formed a ragged circle around the teacher.

'You all did a great job out there,' Ms Maro said as she offered around the oranges. 'Ivy, Tay and Davey, in particular, were wonderful!' Ms Maro's brown eyes sparkled as if she'd just seen a fairy at the bottom of the garden. 'Now we need to stay focused, and remember all those things we've been practising around catching and throwing.'

'Yes, Ms Maro.' The team tried to sound enthusiastic, but everyone knew they'd need a miracle to save this one.

'Now, Sunil, how do you want to set the field?' Ms Maro handed the captain the shiny new ball.

Davey jumped in. 'Can I go deep cover?' he said, wiggling his eyebrows at Sunil. Now that Tay was out of Whopper Chomps, he most definitely wanted to be well out of range of her singing.

Sunil nodded and winked. 'Sure. And Clouter, you're at deep fine leg – over there.' Sunil pointed.

Davey figured his friend was hoping to keep Mo out of earshot of the other team.

Mo nodded. His cheeks were still bulging with lollies and now Davey noticed his pockets were bulging too. There was no way he'd be able to say boo, let alone bother anyone, with those in his mouth.

Sunil quickly set the rest of his field and they all moved to their positions.

'Just pick up your phone and make that call . . .'

As Tay took up her spot behind the batting wicket and Ivy went to stand at first slip, the two girls continued to sing that awful B4U

song. But when at last Davey reached his place at deep cover, he could no longer hear them. He let out a sigh. *Phew*!

Batfish Beach's opening batters wandered out to take their places. Sunil bowled first, starting with a fast good-length ball outside off stump. The batter seemed unsure whether to move forward or back and in the end let it go through to Tay, who caught it effortlessly.

Sunil's second ball seemed to have the same effect: the batter looked fidgety, unsure, and when he tried to make a shot he missed.

By the middle of the second over, the opening batter was out.

When the next Batfish fronted up at the crease, she too seemed unable to find a rhythm. Sunil adjusted his field, ordering everyone in closer – except Davey and Mo – to put further pressure on the Batfish batters.

Soon a second batter was out, for a total of only fourteen runs. And then a third, caught in slips by Ivy Mundine for six.

Out at deep cover, Davey couldn't really see why things were going so badly for the Batfish. Usually, they were strong in the batting department, probably more so than their bowling. But not today.

In the end, the Batfish middle order crumbled like a cupcake and, with just two batters left, they'd scored a measly thirty-two runs.

As their number ten batter came to the crease, Sunil ordered everyone closer. 'Warner!' he called. 'Your turn to bowl!'

Davey raised his eyebrows. He didn't always get a bowl in real matches, but he liked to keep his hand in if he could.

He crossed the field towards the bowler's wicket. As he drew closer, he became aware of the sound of Tay's voice.

'*You're my one, my only bab-by-y-y-y.*'
Clearly she hadn't stopped for the entire time the Batfish had been batting.

Sunil tossed him the ball.

Davey glanced across at Mo, who was now standing at square leg. The great galoot was still sucking on lollies. *His dentist will love him*, Davey thought.

Davey paced out his run-up and marked the spot. He could still hear Tay singing, but for some reason, when he was bowling, it didn't bother him.

He ran in and bowled a leg-spinner. The batter tried to block it and missed. Tay caught it and in a trice the ball was back with Davey.

This time, Davey put more topspin on the ball, causing it to drop quickly and bounce high. The batter misjudged it, moving forward to drive, but hitting it in the air into the covers. Sunil was there to catch it.

'Out!'

The batter trudged off. There was one Batfish left.

'Keep going, Warner!' Sunil gave him the thumbs-up.

'If you care, if you care at all . . .'

Tay was half-humming, half-singing as she once more got into position behind the wicket. It wasn't particularly loud or annoying, Davey realised now, *unless you happened to be batting!* Still, he felt sorry for the Batfish team's last batter.

Davey ran over to Tay. 'Stop singing!' he whispered in her ear.

Tay looked at him in surprise. 'Oh sure! Sorry!'

Davey zipped back to the bowler's end and walked to his mark. He turned and eyed the Batfish batter. Behind the wicket, Tay was silent.

Davey ran in and bowled a googly. The batter thought it was spinning to the off side.

He played at it, but the ball had already turned in the other direction, inside the bat, and it hit the wicket. The bails tumbled.

The Batfish were all out for thirty-two.

CHAPTER 14

THE SANDHILL FLATS SINGERS

'Three cheers for everyone!' Ms Maro
threw her arms wide, her face beaming.
'Hip hip hooray!' everyone shouted as
enthusiastically as they could. Only Mo was
silent, still sucking on a Whopper Chomp.

'Mo, I think you've had enough of those lollies,' Ms Maro said, patting him on the back. 'They're bad for your teeth.'

Mo gulped and swallowed. He looked a little green around the gills. Davey guessed that eighty Whopper Chomps in one afternoon would do that to you.

'Still, you've been quiet as a mouse, haven't you?' Ms Maro flashed Mo a lovely smile.

Davey glanced at Sunil. Ms Maro really *was* cleverer than she let on.

Sunil made as if to wipe his brow. Davey grimaced at his friend in agreement. He still couldn't believe they'd won. Not after everything that had gone wrong.

The team formed two straggly lines and followed Ms Maro back across the park towards school.

As they crossed Flatter Drive, Davey heard the school bell sound. 'So, what happened to McNab, I wonder,' he said.

'Ask him.'

Davey looked up. Sure enough, there was Kevin, wearing dress pants and a red satin shirt.

'How'd you go?' Kevin called as they approached.

'We won, no thanks to you, McNab,' Sunil barked. 'What happened?'

'Spider thing didn't work – at all! Dunno why. Mum just rolled her eyes, grabbed me

by my collar and frog-marched me to the bus stop. It was weird. So I had to dance instead. Sorry.'

He held up the Vegemite jar. 'Here's your spider, Warner, safe and sound.'

Davey took the jar and peered into it. The spider was still playing dead. 'Think I might let him out here. Mum doesn't want him at home.' Davey bent down, unscrewed the lid and shook out the jar. As soon as the spider hit the ground, it scuttled off into the grass.

Ms Maro clapped her hands. 'Now, grab your bags from your classroom and then off you go and have a lovely weekend. You deserve it, guys!'

Davey and his friends set off across the quadrangle towards 6M's room.

Kevin went with them. 'So how did Clouter go?' he said quietly.

'I took care of him.' Tay was just behind them, walking with her new best friend, Ivy.

Sunil and Davey turned to stare at her. 'You?'

'Mo told me he was going to annoy the Batfish and lose us the match. So I gave him all the Whopper Chomps that you gave me, Sunil.' Tay smiled. 'That shut him up.'

Davey nodded. 'Sure did.' He narrowed his eyes. 'But I thought you liked Mo . . .'

'Nah, not really. Shania was right. He's a bit, well, thick.'

'Sure is,' Ivy said. 'For one thing, he hates cricket.'

Tay put her hand in her shorts pocket. 'Here, I saved the last one for you, Davey,' she said, pulling out a Whopper Chomp and handing it to him. 'For getting you into trouble. It should have been me polishing the bowls and sorting the paperclips. Sorry.' She flashed him a wide smile.

Davey shrugged. 'It's okay. Wasn't your fault. Mr Mudge is just a total . . .'

'Mudge!' they all yelled at once.

'Yes?' Mudge had appeared out of nowhere. 'What are you lot doing on school grounds? It's home time. Scoot!' The teacher's ears were already turning magenta.

Without saying anything, everyone ran to the classroom and grabbed their bags.

'Bye, guys!' Tay and Ivy waved before wandering off, arm in arm, singing. *'You're my one, my only, b-a-a-b-b-b-y-y-y!'*

'How could anyone like that song?' Davey frowned. 'And what do they see in that band? Four guys in stupid clothes singing stupid songs in stupid voices. Why do girls like that stuff?'

Sunil grimaced. 'No idea.'

'Nah, me neither,' George said, shrugging. 'It's weird.'

'Totally weird,' Kevin agreed.

They turned and headed for the bike racks. Davey heard a familiar bark. Max was tearing across the playground to meet them.

'War-*ner*!!!' It was Mudge. 'What's that dog doing on school grounds?!!'

'So, why do you reckon the Batfish batting order collapsed like that?' Davey looked across at his best friend. They were lying on the grass out the front, sucking on an ice-block and intermittently throwing balls for Max to chase.

'Gotta thank Tay for that, I think.' Sunil smiled.

Davey took a big bite out of his ice-block and sucked and crunched on it thoughtfully. 'Yeah, well, she's a good wicket-keeper,' he said. 'She's at least as good as Dylan – probably better.'

'She is, but that's not why we won.' Sunil eyed Davey. 'You know how you hate her singing when you're batting? Well, you're not alone. Those Batfish couldn't concentrate.'

'Ah!' Davey had suspected as much. 'So why didn't the umpire tell her to stop?'

''Cause he couldn't really hear her from the other end. It's only annoying if you're batting.'

Max dropped the ball by Davey's hand. It was covered in dog slobber. 'Eeewww!' He picked it up and threw it as far as he could. 'At least Mo couldn't annoy the Batfish,' he said as Max ran off after the ball. 'He was too busy sucking on lollies.'

Davey looked at Sunil. 'And anyway, it's okay to sing, isn't it?'

'Course it is! Especially if you're good at it.'

'Yeah, that's what I thought.' Davey slurped his ice-block loudly. 'And Tay's good at it. She should go on that TV show – *Total Talent Time*.'

'She should,' Sunil said, doing an even louder slurp. 'And I really like that B4U song she sings. It's great.'

'Sure is! I've *always* liked it.' Davey grinned.

'*Just pick up your phone and make that call!*' they sang together in their loudest, most chipmunky voices.

Max looked out from the bushes and howled.

'See? Even Max can sing, the melodious mutt!'

Max howled again. 'Aaahhhooo!'

'Keep it down!' Davey and Sunil shouted.

 **165**